DANNY'S DOODLES

The Dog Biscuit Breakfast

David A. Adler

sourcebooks
jabberwocky

Published by Sourcebooks Jabberwocky, an imprint of Sourcebooks, Inc.
P.O. Box 4410, Naperville, Illinois 60567-4410
(630) 961-3900
Fax: (630) 961-2168
www.sourcebooks.com

Library of Congress Cataloging-in-Publication Data

Adler, David A., author, illustrator.
  Danny's doodles : the dog biscuit breakfast / David A. Adler.
      pages cm
  Summary: The ever-quirky Calvin convinces Danny to help him start a rent-a-pet business when Calvin's Aunt Ruth asks the boys to watch her miniature collie while she is away, but first they will have to find a renter.
  [1. Eccentrics and eccentricities--Fiction. 2. Intellect--Fiction. 3. Friendship--Fiction. 4. Collie--Fiction. 5. Dogs--Fiction. 6. Schools--Fiction.] I. Title. II. Title: Dog biscuit breakfast.
  PZ7.A2615Dak 2014
  [Fic]--dc23

                                      2015002166

Source of Production: Versa Press, East Peoria, Illinois, USA
Date of Production: June 2015
Run Number: 5004196

                    Printed and bound in the United States of America.
                        VP 10 9 8 7 6 5 4 3 2 1

For my grandson Aaron.

Contents

~~~~~~

Chapter 1

MONDAY MORNING—
DEVON AND PARSLEY

"Look at him," my friend Calvin Waffle says.

We're walking to school, and Calvin points to a man walking a dog. He's wearing a bathrobe and slippers. That's what the man is wearing, not Calvin or the dog. Calvin is wearing one red-and-white polka-dot sock and one purple sock. I can see his socks because his pants are a bit short. The dog is wearing a leash and a collar and has lots of short, curly hair.

"I know all about him," Calvin says.

Maybe he does. Calvin's father is a spy. That's what he told me. Maybe Calvin is one too.

Maybe he's spied on Bathrobe Man. Maybe he's spied on lots of people in our neighborhood.

Maybe he's spied on me!

Calvin says, "The man has a child, probably a son named Devon, who wanted a dog. 'I'll take care of him,' Devon promised. 'I'll even

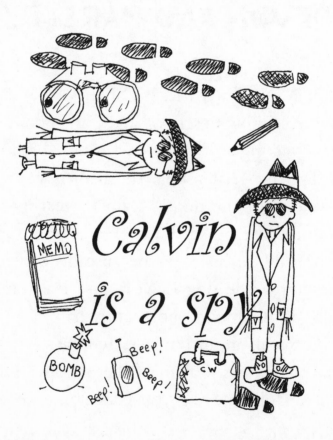

2

clean up after him. Please, Dad, please.'" Calvin stops. He grabs my arm and asks, "And do you know what that man did?"

I shake my head. I don't know. I'm not the spy. Calvin is.

"He bought the dog for his son. Because of all that curly hair, Devon named the dog Parsley, and for the first two weeks, he walked Parsley five times a day. He fed the dog so much that it puked."

"Yuck!"

Just thinking about a dog puking makes me want to puke.

"That was just two weeks ago, and do you know what?"

I shake my head. How should I know what? I didn't even know the boy's name was Devon.

"Now Devon doesn't even look at Parsley. He surely doesn't take care of him."

This is all very interesting, but we have to get to school.

"We've got to get going," I tell Calvin. "We can't be late again."

Our teacher is Mrs. Cakel, and she doesn't like it when we're late. She also doesn't seem to like it when we're on time.

Mrs. Cakel doesn't like it if we write our names too small or too big at the top of our homework papers. She doesn't like it when we answer her questions too loud or too quiet— even if the answer is right. She also doesn't like it if we wear shirts with sparkles or sneakers with blinking lights. Actually, Mrs. Cakel doesn't like most things we do or wear. I don't think she's a happy woman.

Calvin lets go of my arm. We walk toward the corner and then stop. We wait for it to be safe to cross the street.

Calvin turns and says, "Now look at him."

I look at Bathrobe Man

again. He's pulling on Parsley's leash. The dog wants to smell the grass, and Bathrobe Man is in a rush. He looks tired and grumpy.

"Devon no longer wants the dog," Calvin tells me. "Now he wants a football. Now it's Devon's father who feeds, walks, and cleans up after Parsley. He shouldn't have bought his son a dog. He should have rented one."

"You can't rent a dog," I say.

"Why not? You can rent ice skates, boats, chairs for a party, penguin suits, and cars. Why can't you rent a dog?"

"Penguin suits?"

"Tuxedos. You know, the suits men wear to weddings." Calvin thinks for a moment and then tells me, "One day, I might get married, but I won't wear a tuxedo."

We watch as Parsley lifts one of its back legs. I don't want to say what Parsley does, only that I'll be real careful this afternoon when we walk home from school. I don't want to step where that dog stopped and did what it did. I'm wearing sneakers, and it's not easy getting that stuff out of the grooves in the bottoms of sneakers. I tell that to Calvin.

Calvin laughs and says, "Can you imagine, I'm getting married and I'm wearing the shiny shoes people wear with their penguin suits, and I step in that stuff? People would smell me as I walk down the aisle. They wouldn't say 'Here comes the groom.' They'd say 'Here comes the stink.'"

6

I can't imagine that. Not the smelly shoe stuff. I can't imagine Calvin getting married.

I look at my watch again and say, "We've really got to get going."

He doesn't care if Mrs. Cakel yells, but I do.

We cross the street.

As we walk, Calvin keeps talking about Parsley, and all this parsley talk is making me hungry. Mom usually serves parsley on fried fish, and she serves the fish with french fried potatoes, and I love those fries dipped in ketchup.

"We're here," Calvin says.

We are. We're in the school playground and we're on time. Kids are still here waiting for the bell to ring.

My friends Douglas and Annie are right by the door. They have been my friends since kindergarten. Now they're Calvin's friends too.

Douglas and Annie are not by the school door because they're in a hurry to see Mrs. Cakel. It's just that she gives us so much homework and we have to take so many books back and forth to school that our book bags are real heavy. Douglas and Annie are standing by the door because they're in a hurry to put their bags down.

The bell rings.

"I'm going to think about that," Calvin says as we walk into school. "I'm going to think about Devon and his father and that curly-haired dog. I'm going to think about how I can start a rent-a-pet business."

He can't fill his house with dogs and other pets. His mother won't let him have any. I think she's allergic.

Sybil rides again!

Calvin stops by the water fountain. I go right to class.

"There's work on the board," Mrs. Cakel tells us as we walk into class. "Get started."

The whole board is covered with writing. The

heading is "Chronology of the Revolution." Under that is a list of years and things that happened in the time of George Washington.

Did you know that Paul Revere and William Dawes were not the only ones to warn "The British are coming"? Those were both in 1775. Two years later, in 1777, Sybil Ludington, a sixteen-year-old girl, warned that the British were attacking in Danbury, Connecticut. Sybil Ludington rode lots of miles on a horse named Star.

"Mrs. Cakel could just print off the stuff and give it to us, but she writes it on the board and makes us copy it," Douglas once said during lunch. "She does that to keep us busy and quiet."

"No," Annie said. "Copying that stuff helps us remember it."

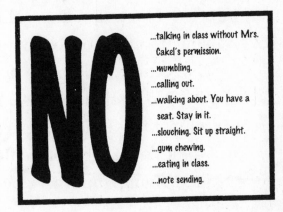

NO
...talking in class without Mrs. Cakel's permission.
...mumbling.
...calling out.
...walking about. You have a seat. Stay in it.
...slouching. Sit up straight.
...gum chewing.
...eating in class.
...note sending.

I don't try to know why Mrs. Cakel tells us to do things. I just do them. That keeps me out of trouble.

BANG!

Calvin drops his book bag on the floor.

PLOP!

He falls into his seat.

Mrs. Cakel looks at him, and it's not an "I'm so glad you're on time today" look. It's more of an "I'll get you" and a "You'll be sorry" look.

I once asked Calvin why he makes so much noise when he comes to class.

"She has that big **NO** sign in the room," he told me. "No talking in class without her permission. No mumbling. No calling out. No walking about. No slouching. No gum chewing. No eating in class. No note sending. It does not say 'No book dropping.' It does not say 'No seat plopping.' That means it's allowed."

"No, it doesn't," I told Calvin. "It doesn't say 'No kite flying,' but that doesn't mean you can bring in a kite with lots of string and fly it in the classroom."

"Kite flying in Cakel's class," Calvin said. "That's a great idea."

If anyone else had said that, I would have known he was joking, but with Calvin, I couldn't be sure.

"I'll need a breeze," Calvin said, "so I'll open all the windows. I'll get a dragon kite with long paper teeth and a long paper tail." He thought for a moment and then added, "I'll start it flying in the classroom, and when it hits the ceiling, I'll push it out the window. I'll tie the end of the string to my desk. Oh, this will be fun!"

I didn't tell Calvin he wouldn't be allowed to fly a kite in class. It's not a good idea to tell Calvin

11

what's not allowed. He thinks of the word *no* as a challenge. That might be why he has so much trouble with Mrs. Cakel. She's always telling us what not to do, and he's always doing it.

So far, he hasn't brought a kite to class. But the school year is not over.

After we copy the chronology, Mrs. Cakel talks to us about the war. She tells us about the winter that began at the end of 1777. George Washington led his troops to Valley Forge, Pennsylvania. It was real cold, and many of his soldiers had no coats or shoes. But they worked like beavers—really like beavers—and built cabins with logs and mud. Washington's wife, Martha, knitted socks for the men. It's too bad she didn't knit shoes and coats for them.

After the American Revolution lesson, Mrs. Cakel teaches us more stuff about fractions. Then we read.

Every few minutes I look at Calvin. He has his book open but I can tell he isn't reading. His eyes aren't moving. Try it. You can't read without moving your eyes.

On our way to lunch, Calvin says, "I've been thinking about Devon and Parsley. I can't have a dog or any pet, but I have figured how I can start a rent-a-pet business."

His idea must have something to do with computers. When he's not thinking about how to upset Mrs. Cakel, he's playing computer games. I bet he's going to create virtual pets. It will be like you have a pet dog, but it will just be on the computer. His idea won't work. A computer can't run to you and wag its tail when you get home from school. You can't pet a computer.

Calvin hasn't told me his idea, just that he has one. I don't know what he's planning, but I think it will lead to trouble. Calvin's ideas usually do.

CALViN, DOUGLAS, ANNie, aND Me

Chapter 2

~~~~~~~~~~~~~~~~~~~~~~~~~~~~~~

IT'S NOT A DREAM.
IT'S A NIGHTMARE.

In the cafeteria, Calvin, Douglas, Annie, and I sit at our regular table, the one nearest the window.

Annie opens her lunch bag. She's got another smelly salami sandwich. Soon it will be nose-holding time. Her breath smells good in the morning, but every day after lunch, she has salami breath.

Calvin has a marshmallow-banana-carrot sandwich on whole wheat bread. He says he doesn't like

it, but he makes his own lunch, so every day he makes himself a sandwich for lunch that he doesn't like. Now, it's hard to explain why Calvin does that, but Calvin is hard to explain.

He also has a bunch of cookie mistakes. His mother works in a bakery, and sometimes the drop of raspberry jelly that should be in the middle of the cookie is way off to the side. That's a cookie mistake and they can't sell it, so his mother brings it home. He also has lots of broken cookies that they can't sell. And do you know what? Cookie mistakes and broken cookies taste just as good as regular ones.

Douglas has bologna. I know bologna looks

and tastes like salami, but it doesn't smell the same. I have American cheese and lettuce.

"Listen to this," Calvin says. He tells Douglas and Annie all about Devon, Bathrobe Man, and Parsley.

"Now listen to my great idea."

I know I shouldn't listen, but I do. Somehow I feel his idea will mean trouble for me.

I should tell him I can't get involved with any idea he has, that I have to help Martha Washington knit socks for the Continental Army.

But I don't.

I should tell him I have to hurry because I'm going on a ride with Sybil Ludington.

But I don't.

I listen to Calvin's great idea.

"Here it is. Children want pets, but after one or two weeks, they're bored with them. Danny and I are starting a new business, Calvin's Rent-A-Pet."

"Hey," I say. "If we're in business together, why is it just called Calvin's? What about me?"

"Okay, Calvin and Danny's Rent-A-Pet."

"That's better."

Calvin stands. He's about to announce his great idea.

"There's a real need for pets that dads and moms can rent. That's the whole idea behind Calvin and Danny's Rent-A-Pet. But where do we get the pets? I can't keep them in my house. My mom's allergic."

I told you!

I hope he doesn't plan to keep animals at my house. My mom doesn't like a mess. She likes our house to be neat and clean, and that means no animals.

"People travel," Calvin says, "and they can't take their pets with them. What do they do?

18

They pay a lot of money for someone to watch their dogs and cats and ferrets."

Ferrets?

"Now they can bring their pets to Calvin and Danny's Rent-A-Pet and pay just a little. What will we do with all those pets?"

That's a rhetorical question, the kind you don't answer.

"We won't keep the pets. We'll rent them to lots of people like Bathrobe Man so they won't have to buy dogs for their children. They can rent one for just a week or two. By the time their children are bored with their pets, they'll give them back to us and we'll return them to their real owners, who will be back from their trips."

"Hey," Douglas says. "That *is* a good idea."

"It's a *great* idea," Calvin says.

He says *great* much too loud. He kinda shouts it. Kids from the other tables turn and look.

"People who give us their pets because they're traveling will pay us. People who rent the pets will pay us. Everyone will be paying us."

Hey, I'll be rich.

Calvin talks on and on about his idea.

"Danny and I will advertise for people who travel to leave their pets with us. We'll also put signs near pet shops: 'Don't buy your child a pet. Rent one!' Soon it will be big, big business. We'll make so much money that we'll buy the school and fire the Cakel."

WE'LL BUY THE SCHOOL!

I don't like the way that sounds, especially the "we'll" part. Why would I want to own a school?

How did this happen? How did I get involved in all this?

Now I remember. I complained when he called his business just Calvin's Rent-A-Pet.

Douglas says, "I want to be in the business."

Calvin looks at me.

"We're not ready to hire workers," he says. Then he asks me, "Isn't that right?"

"I don't know," I answer. "I don't know anything. I don't even know how I became a partner in a pet-renting business and in buying a school."

"You're my best friend," Calvin tells me. "I couldn't do this without you."

What can I say?

Lunchtime ends. We go back to class, and I keep thinking about this Rent-A-Pet idea and wonder what's wrong with it. I haven't known Calvin real long. It's only been two months since he moved onto my block. I like him, but I'm not sure I want to be his business partner. His idea sounds good, but somehow I know it will lead to trouble, and I'll be in the middle of it.

"Daniel."

It's Mrs. Cakel. She's calling on me.

"Well, what's the answer?"

The answer? I don't even know the question.

"I don't know."

"You've been dreaming all afternoon."

I haven't been paying attention, but I'm not dreaming. This Rent-A-Pet business is not a dream. It's more of a nightmare.

Mrs. Cakel walks to my desk. She looks down at me and says, "I'm teaching a science lesson on magnets. I asked if a magnet would stick to your desk."

"Oh."

"Well, would it?"

"It would stick to the metal legs but not to the wooden top."

"Thank you," she says. "And Danny, for homework, since you missed the lesson, write a one-page report on magnets."

A report!

Extra homework!

I blame Calvin for this. But it doesn't matter who I blame. I'm the one who has to do the report.

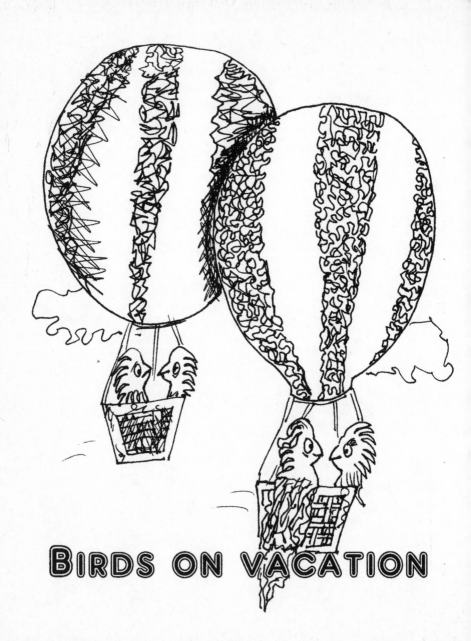

BIRDS ON VACATION

Chapter 3

~~~~~~~~~~~~~~~~~~~~~~~~~~~

TELEVISION IS
LIKE CAKE

The bell rings. It's time to go home and write about magnets.

I gather my books. I just take the ones I need for homework and leave the others in my desk. That's not what Calvin does. He doesn't want to think about which ones he needs, so he takes them all, and lots of times, when he gets home, he doesn't look at any of them. Lots of times he doesn't do the homework.

"Daniel, I want to speak with you."

Mrs. Cakel said that.

What did I do now?

I take my books and go to Mrs. Cakel's desk. Calvin comes with me.

"I only asked for Daniel," Mrs. Cakel says.

The school day is over. I don't think she wants to see any more of him until tomorrow. Maybe she doesn't *ever* want to see any more of him. It's okay being Calvin's friend, but I wouldn't want to be his teacher.

Calvin tells her, "Danny and I walk home together."

She gives me a large envelope.

"Evan broke his ankle."

I knew that. He was absent.

"This is his homework. I think you pass his house on your way home."

I smile and tell her we do, that we'll bring Evan the homework. Mrs. Cakel doesn't smile back. She's not a smiley person.

As we walk out of the building, Calvin tells me, "It's just not fair. I dream of missing school, a whole day with no work. Evan is living my dream, but the Cakel ruins it. She sends him stuff to do at home."

Calvin says, "I wouldn't do homework if I were home with a broken ankle. I wouldn't do homework if I were home with a broken toe or finger or arm. I wouldn't do homework if I were home with laryngitis or bronchitis or any itis-titis disease."

I'm sure that's true.

We get to Evan's house, and I ring the bell.

"Hello, Danny," his mother says as she opens the door. She's holding Evan's baby sister who was born while we were in third grade. We're in fourth grade now.

"This is Calvin," I tell her. "He's also in our class."

"Hello, Calvin," she says. "Evan is in his room. He's waiting for you."

We follow her up the stairs to Evan's bedroom. He's lying on his bed, on lots of pillows, so he's more sitting than lying. His right foot is a big white plaster cast. At the foot of his bed, on a stand, is an enormous television set. Evan is holding a remote.

"Wow!" Calvin says. "That's some big television."

"My parents rented it so I'd have something to do while I'm home."

"You see," Calvin says. "You can rent just about anything."

He tells Evan his Rent-A-Pet idea.

Evan says, "I want a cat, but my parents say I'm not ready to take care of one, but do you know what?"

28

That's another of those rhetorical questions, the kind you don't answer.

"Cats take care of themselves. You don't walk them. They make potty in the house, in a litter box. You don't have to bathe them because they lick themselves clean. And they're easy to feed. You just open cans of cat food and dump it in a bowl."

That does sound easy.

"Here's what you do," Calvin tells him. "Ask your parents to rent you a cat from Calvin and Danny's Rent-A-Pet. You'll have one for two weeks, and you'll prove you can take care of it."

Evan says, "I'll ask them while they still feel bad for me because of my ankle. Since I fell off my bike and broke my ankle, my

parents have let me have just about whatever I want."

That's how he broke it!

I've fallen off my bike lots of times, but I never broke an ankle or leg or anything. Once I fell with my sunglasses in my pocket. I fell right on them, but they didn't break. I guess I'm lucky.

Evan asks us about school. He even asks about Mrs. Cakel. He misses her.

Calvin asks, "How can you miss the Cakel?"

"I got used to her rules. That was easy. But I can't get used to lying in bed all day and watching television."

"Watching television all day sounds easy to me," Calvin says. "I could get used to that."

Evan shakes his head.

"Television is like cake," he says. "If you had boxes and boxes of cake and could eat as much of it as you want, at some point, you'd be full and not want anymore. Right now I'm full of cartoons and comedies and game shows."

Calvin looks at me and says, "You're smiling. What do you think? Could you ever have too much cake or television?"

"I don't know," I answer. "But for once, I'd like to be the one to decide when I've had enough instead of my mother saying, 'That's your last piece of cake. You've had enough. Turn off the TV. You've watched enough.'"

Calvin says, "My mom never tells me I've had enough cake. She has a job at the bakery. She's the one who uses a hypodermic needle and shoots jelly into jelly donuts.

"That's such a great job," Evan says.

He makes his hand into a pretend gun and shoots it.

"*Bang! Bang!*" Evan says. "I'm shooting jelly."

Calvin says, "Mom brings home messed-up cakes and broken cookies from work and almost forces me to eat them. She tells me it would be a waste to throw them out."

I tell Evan, "If you're tired of television, maybe you should read. I can loan you some of my baseball books. I'll bring them tomorrow."

I give him the homework envelope.

I'm ready to go, but Evan keeps talking. I guess he doesn't want us to leave. At last, Calvin and I say good-bye.

On our way home, Calvin says, "Maybe I should break my ankle and stay home from school."

That sounds like one of those things kids say but don't really mean. You don't respond to those things. They are like rhetorical questions. Who would intentionally break his ankle so he could miss school?

Calvin might.

He has strange ideas.

"You don't want to do that," I tell him. "Breaking a bone can hurt, and it could keep you from running real fast. You'll hit the ball but won't be able to beat the throw to first base."

"I don't play baseball."

"You might be running for another reason. You might do something so wrong that Mrs. Cakel will chase after you, and because you broke your ankle, she'll catch you."

"Yeah, I don't want that."

We're in front of Calvin's house. I say good-bye to him. I walk home, and all the way, I worry that Calvin will intentionally break his ankle.

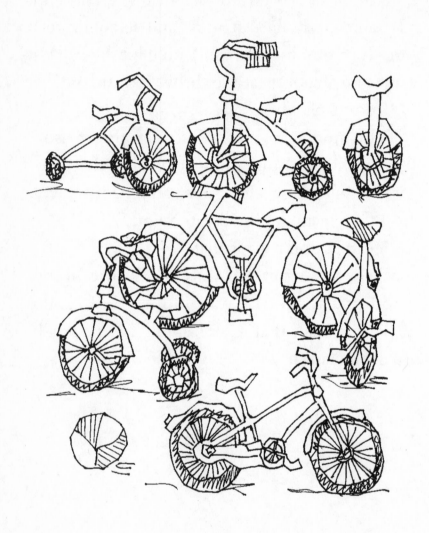

Chapter 4

NOODLING

"I have a surprise for you," Dad says when I walk in the house.

I wait.

No surprise.

"I'll give it to you after dinner."

Dad smiles. But that's it. He doesn't even hint what he's giving me after dinner. I have no time to think about it. I have lots of math and history homework to do and a report on magnets.

Believe me, when I do the math homework, I'm tempted to just make up answers. But I don't. I'm not Calvin.

I answer all the history questions.

Did you know that Benjamin Franklin gave George Washington his gold-topped walking stick?

Did you know that George Washington had slaves? In his last will, he freed them all. I know he waited until he died to free them, but for his slaves, that was a great thing. They were free. Where Washington lived, most people left their farms and houses *and* slaves to their children, like the slaves were just another "thing" they owned. And Washington left money for any of the slaves who were too old or too sick to take care of themselves.

Some history is interesting.

I research magnets on the Internet.

Did you know that magnets are not attracted to all metals? They don't stick to aluminum. Magnets stick to the metal nickel but not to the five-cent nickel. That's because the coin is mixed with copper, and magnets don't stick to copper.

I write the magnet report on my computer and set the font at fourteen so I quickly fill one page.

Mom calls me to dinner—fried fish with parsley, french fries, and broccoli.

Broccoli pieces are like small trees, and Mom makes me eat at least three small trees.

Dad asks, "Are you wondering about the surprise?"

Of course I am.

But I think Dad's question is rhetorical, so I don't answer.

"It's a unicycle," he says. "It's in the garage."

"Hey, I've always wanted to ride one of those."

"I know."

Dad works at a bicycle and exercise equipment store. That must be where he got it.

A tricycle has three wheels and is easy to ride. A bicycle has two wheels and is not so easy to ride. A unicycle has just one wheel. I wonder how difficult it will be to ride a unicycle.

"Go ahead and look at it," Mom tells us. "I'll save you some dessert."

Dad and I go to the garage. On the way, he tells me that his boss gave him the unicycle. He had two in his shop for a few years, and they have not sold. People look at them, but they don't buy them. He thinks keeping one would be enough.

Dad opens the garage door.

There it is, just one wheel, pedals, and a seat.

"Try it first on the grass," he says, "so you won't hurt yourself when you fall."

When I fall?

Why does Dad think I'll fall?

Dad takes it outside. He stands it up on the front lawn. He holds it there and tells me, "Get on and try it."

I climb on. There's nothing on the unicycle to hold on to, so I hold on to Dad. I stretch my feet down to the pedals.

"Let go," I tell Dad.

Dad lets go.

I fall.

I try it again and again and keep falling. I don't know how anyone can ride one of these things.

Dad holds it for me. I get up, sit on the seat, and put each foot on a pedal. Dad counts to three. At *three* he lets go. I pedal, but before I can get the unicycle to move, I fall.

"That's enough for today," Dad says.

Enough? All I did was sit and fall. But Dad is right. It's enough. We take the unicycle into the garage again and go back in the house. Mom and Karen are still in the dining room eating oranges and grapes. That's dessert, navel oranges and seedless green grapes.

"How did it go?" Mom asks.

"It's not easy," Dad tells her. "Danny needs to work at it."

Karen tells me, "You also need to learn how to juggle. That's what people do on a unicycle. They juggle."

Karen tosses an orange to me. I catch it. She tosses another one, and I catch it too. She tosses me a third one. I drop the first two and catch the third.

"That's not juggling," Karen tells me. "That's bungling. That's goofing. That's noodling."

"What's noodling?"

"I don't know what noodling is, and I don't know what you just did."

That's my sister, Karen. The English language does not have enough words for her to use to make fun of me, so she has to invent new ones.

I pick the two oranges up off the floor.

I can't ride a unicycle and I can't juggle. I don't feel real good about myself. I take the three oranges and go down to the basement to practice.

Just so you understand—I *know* how to juggle. I just need to keep one orange in the air as I move the other two from one hand to the next.

I *know* how to juggle. I just can't do it.

First, I try to hold all three oranges. That means one in one hand and two in the other. Maybe that's the problem. They're too big. I can't hold two in one hand.

I throw up one orange.

I threw it up too high. It hits the ceiling, falls, and hits my head.

I try again. This time, I don't throw it up so high. I quickly throw up another orange and try to catch the first one while I move the third orange from my right hand to my left.

Bam!

An orange hits my head again.

I can't do this.

Maybe I should try juggling something smaller, something easier to catch.

Eggs.

No, not raw eggs. Hard-boiled eggs. We

always have lots of hard-boiled eggs in the refrigerator. When she goes to work, Mom takes them for lunch.

But I won't juggle eggs today. I'll do it tomorrow.

Chapter 5

CALVIN JUGGLES

It's Tuesday morning, and I remembered to bring baseball books for Evan. With the extra books, my bag is really heavy.

I wait for Calvin in front of his house. I always wait for him. If he doesn't hurry, we'll be late.

His front door opens.

Now this is what gets me so angry. He comes out as if he's not late at all. He slowly locks the front door and even more slowly walks to me.

"Let's go," I tell him. "We don't want to be late again."

"Again? We weren't late yesterday. We were on time three days last week."

"And we were late two days," I tell him.

"Being on time is a bad habit," he says. "That's what's wrong with the Cakel. She's encouraging us to form too many bad habits."

I don't argue with Calvin.

"Look what I printed."

He stops and takes some papers from his book bag. They're signs advertising Calvin and Danny's Rent-A-Pet.

"I thought we would tack them on trees on our way to school. But since you're in such a hurry, we'll do it on our way home."

He gives me one sign to look at.

"I'll read it later," I say and fold it and put it in my pocket. "Right now, we have to get to school."

We walk, and I tell him about the unicycle and the trouble I had riding it and trying to juggle.

"Juggling is easy," Calvin says.

He stops, takes three cookie mistakes from his lunch, and juggles them. He catches one in his mouth and eats it. He catches another in his mouth and eats that one too. He catches the last one in his hand and gives it to me. I eat this one.

Calvin can juggle!

Sometimes he amazes me.

Calvin says he'll teach me how.

We start walking again. We get to school, and the playground is empty. We're late.

I dread going past Mrs. Cakel on my way into class. She won't scream at me. She won't say anything. She'll just squeeze her eyes together and wrinkle her nose like she just smells something bad.

I hurry through the hall. Calvin doesn't. He stops at the water fountain and takes a drink.

"Go ahead," he tells me. "I'm still thirsty."

I hurry past Mrs. Cakel. I sit, take out my notebook, and begin to copy the homework assignment from the board.

"Hello, Mrs. Cakel."

It's Calvin. He smiles as he slowly walks past her and into the room.

Have you seen that cartoon on television where a dog is chasing a cat and the cat climbs a tree and the dog can't get it? The dog looks real angry in the cartoon. Smoke is coming out of its ears. Well, that's how Mrs. Cakel looks, like smoke is coming out of her ears.

Cats and dogs! That reminds me of the sign I folded and put in my pocket. Mrs. Cakel is writing something on the board. Her back is to me. I take out the sign and unfold it in my lap.

The headline says, "Dog for Rent." Then it describes the dog, a miniature collie, and the dates it's available.

Where did Calvin get a dog?

The sign also has lots of words about all the animals Calvin and Danny's Rent-A-Pet will board and rent. At the bottom are two telephone numbers. One is Calvin's cell phone number. The other one is my telephone number, only I don't have a cell phone. It's my house phone. It's my parents' and Karen's number too.

Someone might call my house, and Karen will answer it. She'll say, "We have an annoying ferret you can rent. It's name is Danny."

You think I'm joking, but I'm not. Whenever I'm watching a show she doesn't like and won't let her change the channel, that's what she calls me, an annoying ferret.

If Mom answers the phone, she would say, "We don't have any animals here. Animals are dirty."

I don't know what Dad would say, but I do know I've got to get my telephone number off the signs.

"Danny, do your work," Mrs. Cakel calls out.

I look up. Her back is still to me. How does she know I'm not doing my work?

I'm not like Calvin. I don't want to upset Mrs. Cakel, so I do my work. All through the rest of the morning, I look right at Mrs. Cakel, like I'm concentrating on whatever she's saying, only sometimes I'm thinking about Calvin's rent-a-pet business. No, that's not right. It's not just Calvin's business. It's mine too, and that's the problem.

At lunch, I ask Calvin about the dog.

"His name is Mitchell. It's my aunt's dog. She's going somewhere. I think to visit some friends. She's leaving on Thursday, and she said I could have Mitchell while she's away."

"She expects you to watch him and not rent him to some stranger."

"How do you know that?" Calvin asks. "You don't even know my aunt."

Annie unwraps her sandwich, and I smell the salami. How does she eat that stuff?

"I bet you don't even know my aunt's name."

"You're right. I don't know your aunt, and I don't know her name. I just know that when she asked you to watch Mitchell, she doesn't want you to give him to someone else."

"I'm not *giving* him to anyone. I'm *renting* him, and my aunt's name is Ruth."

"Eat your lunch," Annie tells me.

"And there's another thing. You have my telephone number on your signs. What if someone calls to rent a pet and my mother answers the phone?"

"She'll take a message."

"Calvin," Douglas asks, "do you have any extra cookie mistakes?"

Calvin gives him a few cookie mistakes and a funny-shaped jelly donut.

"Your telephone number is at the very bottom of the sign," Calvin tells me. "I'll just tear it off."

Annie has celery stalks for lunch. She says they're filled with vitamins and minerals.

Maybe they are, but they're noisy. Salami and celery—a smelly, noisy lunch.

I finish eating, throw away my sandwich wrappers and other stuff, and we go back to class.

It's a good afternoon. Mrs. Cakel doesn't tell anyone to sit up, speak up, or wake up. After class, she gives me Evan's homework. She tells me to ask Evan when he thinks he'll be coming back to school.

On our way, Calvin and I stop by a tree. He takes a small hammer, a box of metal tacks, and a sign from his bag. I hold the sign against the tree and he tacks it on. We do that again and again on our way to Evan's house. We tack up five or six before I remember the telephone numbers.

"Hey, you left my number on the signs."

"My number is first. People always call the first number."

I cross out my number on the rest of the signs before we tack them up.

We get to Evan's house, and he's glad to see us. I give him the baseball books, and he thanks me.

Evan is even glad to get the homework. He says he'll be back in school on Monday.

I tell Evan about my unicycle, and Calvin demonstrates his juggling. He tears three sheets of paper from his notebook, makes three paper balls, and juggles them.

Calvin says, "I'm going to teach Danny how to juggle."

Evan gets all excited.

"That's great. There's a talent show every Sunday in the children's ward at my hospital. You and Danny can be in it."

"Sure," Calvin says. "We'll be there."

"Hey! I still can't ride a unicycle and I can't juggle."

"Today is just Tuesday. You'll juggle by Sunday. I'm a great juggler and a great teacher."

You're shaking your head, aren't you? You

don't think Calvin is a great teacher. Well, I agree with you. He's not a great student, and I'm sure he's not a great teacher.

Chapter 6

~~~~~~~~~~~~~~~~~~~~~~~~~~~~~~~~~~~~~~

MY TEACHER
THE WAFFLE

"You're going to be a great juggler," Calvin tells me as we walk home. We get to his house, and he says, "Your first lesson is now."

Calvin opens the door and his mother is standing right there with a plate of cookie mistakes.

"I saw you coming," she says, "and I thought you could use a snack before you start your homework."

We follow her to the kitchen. She puts the cookies on the small table. She pours us each a cup of milk and tells us, "Milk is good for you. It's good for your bones, nerves, muscles, and tissues. I'm talking about the tissues in your bodies, not the tissues in a box that you use when you have a cold."

Calvin's mother is an interesting woman. She talks like a runaway train. Just now, she

started talking about milk. I wonder where she'll end up.

"Tissues are more sanitary than handkerchiefs.

My dad always had a fancy handkerchief in his jacket pocket, folded, pointy, and sticking out, but we always said it was for showing and not blowing, and it always matched his necktie. His name was Calvin. He was so proud when we named our son after him. Yes, my dad was Calvin too."

Mrs. Waffle laughs.

"The way I said that it sounded like my dad was the second Calvin but he wasn't. I was using the *too* that means also, not the *two* that's a number. Why do they do that—have so many words in English that sound the same but mean different things?"

You see? She started talking about milk and ended with words that sound the same but have different meanings. I think they're called "homonyms."

Calvin and I eat a few cookie mistakes and drink some milk.

"Mom," my friend Calvin says. "We have a lot to do."

"Yes, I know. Your teacher gives lots of homework. That's one of the things I like about my job at the bakery. I don't get homework."

I follow Calvin to his room. There's not much furniture, just a bed, a nightstand, and a dresser. He takes some small beanbag balls from his dresser and tosses one to me. It's easy to catch. He tosses another. I drop the first ball and catch the second. He tosses another and another beanbag ball to me. I keep dropping one and catching the next.

"At least you know how to catch," Calvin says. "Now I'll teach you how to juggle."

Calvin picks up the beanbags and puts them on his bed.

"Do what I do," he says.

Calvin takes one beanbag ball from the bed. Using just one hand, he tosses it up and catches it again and again. That's what I do.

"Higher," Calvin tells me. "It should go up to nose level, and you should not be looking at the ball. You should be looking straight ahead."

It's not so easy to catch a ball without looking at it, but I keep practicing.

Now Calvin does it with two balls, one with each hand. He throws one ball up and when it's about up to his nose, he throws up the second ball and catches the first, and he keeps doing that. That's what I try to do, but mostly I throw the balls up, and they fall to the floor.

Calvin gets a third ball. He juggles all three, and I just watch.

"Wait right here," he says.

He leaves the room and comes back with an apple. Now he juggles two balls and the apple, and each time he catches the apple, he takes a bite of it. I sit on his bed and watch until he's eaten the entire apple.

I try one more time to throw two balls up in the air at the same time and catch them. I can't do it.

"I'll never be able to juggle."

"Yes, you will. You've got a great teacher. And I don't mean the Cakel. I mean the Waffle."

Calvin gives me three of the beanbag balls and tells me to practice. "That's your homework."

"What about Mrs. Cakel's homework? Let's do it together."

"I'll do it later."

No, he won't.

"Right now," Calvin says, "I'm going to practice some new juggling tricks."

I tell Calvin it's time for me to go home, and he walks with me to the front door.

"Good-bye," I tell Mrs. Waffle, "and thanks for the snack."

"Yes, good-bye. And this week, there's a good buy at the bakery. Three mini jelly donuts for a dollar."

I walk home, and as soon as I open the door, my sister Karen yells at me, "Since when do you have a dog?"

"I don't have a dog."

"Two people called and asked about a miniature collie. They want to rent it."

"Mitchell?"

"No. The people who called are Mildred Foster and Jared Derby."

I follow Karen into the kitchen, and she shows me the note she wrote with their telephone numbers.

"I told them we don't have a miniature collie, and if we did, it wouldn't be for rent."

I tell her about Calvin and Danny's Rent-A-Pet, Calvin's Aunt Ruth, and her dog Mitchell.

Karen laughs.

"You know this is going to end badly. Mitchell might bite someone or run away, and you'll be responsible. He might get fleas, and then so will you. You'll be scratching and scratching until your skin is covered with red splotches. That all *might* happen and it might not, but one thing I know for sure:

you'll get into real trouble, and I'll be here to see it all."

She laughs again and says, "This will be fun."

I don't like that Karen is happy about my troubles, but I think she's right. This whole Rent-A-Pet business will end badly.

Karen watches as I try to juggle the beanbags. After a while, I think the beanbags know when I throw them in the air that they'll soon be on the floor.

Karen tells me, "You're not very good at juggling beanbags."

I know that.

"I'll try something smaller," I say. "I'll try juggling Mom's hard-boiled eggs."

"I'll get them," Karen says.

Karen takes three of Mom's eggs from the refrigerator and puts them on the table. With just my right hand, I throw one egg up just a bit and catch it. I do that again and again. Now I do it with my left hand.

"Throw them higher," Karen says. "Juggle them."

I hold two eggs in my left hand and one in my right hand. I throw one from my left hand, and when it's in the air, I throw the one in my right hand, and then quickly the one still in my left hand.

The first one falls on the floor and breaks.

"Hey!"

The next two fall and break.

"Hey! These aren't Mom's hard-boiled eggs."

"No," Karen laughs. "They're *your* broken eggs."

What a mess!

"I should probably help you clean this up," Karen says. "But I won't. I have homework to do."

Here I am with three broken eggs on the floor and lots of Cakel homework to do.

Isn't life great?

That's another rhetorical question.

Chapter 7

~~~~~~~~~~~~~~~~~~~~~~~~~~~~~~~

I'LL BE A
MILLIONAIRE

Now it's after dinner. I call Calvin and tell him about Mildred Foster and Jared Derby.

"Great!" Calvin says. "Call and tell them Mitchell will be ready Thursday afternoon."

"They'll want to know more than just that. They'll want me to tell them about the dog. They'll want to know if we will bring him to them or if they have to pick him up, and how much the rent will be."

"The rent. That's a good question," Calvin says. "How much should we charge?"

Calvin is quiet for a minute. I guess he's thinking.

"We could charge by the pound," he says. "We could weigh Mitchell and charge fifty cents a pound for each day."

"No," I tell him. "Ferrets weigh almost nothing. If we charge by the pound, we'll get almost no money for renting a ferret. And how would we weigh a parakeet or a goldfish?"

Calvin says, "Mitchell is a good dog. We'll charge four dollars a day for him. How does that sound?"

I say, "That sounds like twenty-eight dollars a week. That's fourteen dollars for me. That sounds great."

I tell Calvin I'll go to his house after I finish my homework. We'll call together.

"Don't spend too much time on your

homework," Calvin tells me. "Remember, the Cakel tells us to do it. She doesn't tell us to do it well. The answers don't have to be right."

That's Calvin. That's not me.

It takes me a while to do it all. I finish and tell Mom I'm going to Calvin's. I get to his house, and Mrs. Waffle opens the door.

"Hello again," she says. "Do you want more cookies? Do you want more milk for your nerves and tissues?"

"No, thank you. I just want to see Calvin."

"He's in his room. I think he's doing his homework."

"Take a look," Calvin says when I get to his room. He shows me his homework. All his answers are wrong.

He likes to be the bad boy. What he doesn't want is for me to tell him his work is "very nice," so that's exactly what I say. Maybe if people don't make a fuss when he gets all the wrong answers, he'll try to get the right answers.

"Let's call those two people," Calvin says.

We're sitting on Calvin's bed. I give him Karen's note with the names and numbers of the people who called. On his cell phone, Calvin presses the buttons for Mildred Foster and gives me the phone.

"You talk," he says. "You're better with adults."

A woman answers the phone.

"Hello. I'm Danny Cohen of Calvin and Danny's Rent-A-Pet."

"Yes," the woman says. "I want to rent that little collie. My nephew will be visiting with me, and he loves animals. Is the dog good with children?"

"My partner Calvin

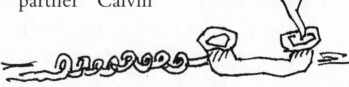

Waffle knows the dog. You can ask him all your questions."

I try to give Calvin the phone, but he shakes his head. He doesn't want to talk.

I tell him her question.

"Tell her that Mitchell is great with children."

"This is Danny again," I tell Mildred Foster. "The dog's name is Mitchell, and he's very good with children."

I tell her what the rent will be and that we'll bring the dog to her house Thursday afternoon. Calvin tells me and I tell her what Mitchell likes to eat. She gives me her address, and I write it on Karen's note.

That's it!

We're in business.

Starting Thursday, I'll be earning two dollars a day. That's my share of the rent.

"What about Jared Derby?" I ask.

"You have to call and tell him the dog has already been rented."

Calvin is lucky to have me as his partner. I don't mind talking to adults.

Jared Derby wants the dog for his son.

"He's eleven and thinks he's ready to be responsible for another living thing. I disagree, so this rent-a-pet thing is a perfect opportunity for him to prove himself."

I tell Mr. Derby that the dog is no longer available.

On the way home, I think that, over a full year, making two dollars a day adds up to $730.

I'm good at math.

After 1,370 years, that's over one million dollars. Wow! In 1,370 years, I'll be a millionaire.

Chapter 8

SHE HAS HER WAYS

On our way to school this morning, all Calvin wants to talk about is our pet business.

"I was right," he says. "There's a real need for pets you can rent. Our problem will be getting the animals. You should tell your parents you want a pet dog, cat, and ferret. You'll train them to be good with strangers, and we'll rent them out."

"No, it's not going to happen," I tell him. "And you should let your aunt know that you won't be watching her dog."

Calvin stops walking. We are still two blocks from school. He turns to me and says, "Do you think if my aunt really cares who watches her dog, she would let me do it? Everyone knows I'm irresponsible."

"Not everyone knows that."

"Sure, some school teacher in Tibet doesn't know it, but everybody else does."

"I don't think you're irresponsible. I just think you're different. That's one of the reasons I like you."

"It is?"

"Yes, it is."

We start walking again.

I've had enough business talk.

"It's Wednesday," I tell Calvin, "and by Sunday, I'm supposed to be riding my unicycle and juggling."

"That's why I brought beanbags to school. You'll practice at lunch."

We get to school. We're on time today, and I know what that means. Tomorrow Calvin will make sure we're late.

Mrs. Cakel checks my homework and hardly looks at it. Now she's checking Calvin's.

"I can't give you credit for this," she says. "Every answer is wrong."

"But I did it," Calvin tells her. "I did my homework."

She taps his notebook with her pen and says, "This is not homework. It's nonsense, and it's not acceptable. You'll have to stay in class during lunch and do it then."

Every answer is wrong!

Calvin looks at her. I know he wants to argue, but you don't argue with Mrs. Cakel. Even Calvin knows that.

Missing lunch with us is a real punishment for Calvin. It's his favorite time of the school day, and he'll hate spending it with Mrs. Cakel.

Morning classes are boring, so I doodle. That's pretty much all I do in school. Soon I'll need a new doodle notebook. This one is almost filled.

The lunch bell rings, and Calvin gives me three beanbag balls and tells me to practice.

"Poor Calvin," Douglas says at lunch. "How bad could his homework be?"

I don't answer. I assume this is another of those rhetorical things.

"Really," Douglas asks, "how bad could it be?"

The question isn't rhetorical, so I answer it.

"Calvin purposely wrote the wrong answers. Listen to what he wrote for the one about who was on the committee to write the Declaration of Independence."

Annie says, "I know the answer."

She's the opposite of Calvin. Her hand is always up in class, and she would never give the wrong answer on purpose.

"Thomas Jefferson," Annie says, "John

Adams, Benjamin Franklin, Roger Sherman, and Robert Livingston."

Annie already ate part of her sandwich, so with every name, I get a whiff of her salami breath.

"That's not what Calvin wrote," I say. "He wrote, 'Not me. I get too much homework to be on any committee.' And for the math questions, he just made up numbers."

Douglas says, "We do get a lot of homework. If this was 1775, and Paul Revere rode by my house and said, 'The British are coming,' I'd have to say, 'Tell them to wait. I'm doing homework.'"

Let's ride!

81

I eat my sandwich and pretzels. Then I tell Douglas and Annie about my unicycle and the hospital talent show. I show them the beanbag balls.

"Can you juggle them?" Douglas asks.

"Not yet. Calvin is teaching me how, and he wants me to practice."

I sip some milk and then take a beanbag ball in my right hand and toss it up, catch it, and toss it up again. I keep doing this while I take a ball in my left and do the tossing thing. Now I'm tossing two beanbag balls at the same time. I don't want to drop them, so I don't toss them too high.

I try tossing the one in my right hand to my left hand and the other one to my right hand.

Douglas and Annie are watching.

The first few times when I make the switch from one hand to the other, I drop the balls. But now I'm catching them.

"Hey, you're juggling," Annie shouts.

I'm only catching two balls with two hands. I think I'd have to be tossing and catching three balls to be really juggling.

A few kids come to our table to watch. Having an audience is making me a bit nervous, but I keep at it.

"Hey, everybody!" Douglas shouts. "Danny's juggling."

Now a few more kids and Mr. Baker, the cafeteria aide, are watching.

"He's only throwing two beanbags," someone calls out. "That's not really juggling."

I agree.

Mr. Baker leaves the group, leans into the

microphone, and says, "Clean your tables. Lunch period will be over in two minutes."

I stop juggling, quickly finish my milk, and throw away my wrappers, empty milk container, and lunch bag. The bell rings, and we go back to class.

Annie is the first in the room. "Danny can juggle," she tells Calvin.

"He has a good teacher," Calvin says, but he doesn't look happy.

Calvin whispers to me, "I spent the whole period doing my homework and looking at that."

He points to Mrs. Cakel.

"Stop complaining," Mrs. Cakel says.

She's writing on the board. She's not even looking at us. Calvin leans close to me and whispers real low, "How did she hear me?"

I have my ways.

84

SHE HAS HER WAYS

Mrs. Cakel turns, faces Calvin, and tells him, "I have my ways."

When she heard him, she wasn't facing us. Calvin was whispering real low. Mrs. Cakel sure does have her ways. She knows everything that happens in her classroom.

The afternoon science lesson is on magnets again, about how they are used in all kinds of machines. I know all this stuff. It was in my report.

I look straight at Mrs. Cakel. I want her to think I'm listening. While I'm looking, I'm doodling. I can't help it. My right hand doodles even without me thinking about it.

"Daniel."

Mrs. Cakel calls me that when she's angry. Otherwise, she calls me Danny.

"How do we use magnets?"

She expects me to repeat what she just told us, how magnets are used in televisions, computers, and microwave ovens. I don't. Instead, I tell her things she hasn't said.

"MRI machines in hospitals use magnets to take pictures of people's bodies to figure out if they're sick or not. Magnets are used to slow down trains."

"Yes, very good, Danny. Now stop doodling."

I'm listening. Why does she care if I'm doodling?

I put my pen down and close my notebook. That will keep my right hand from doodling and getting me in trouble.

The bell finally rings. The school day is done. I'm glad. I like learning new things, but sometimes it's a real struggle to pay attention.

Mrs. Cakel gives me a large envelope of work for Evan.

"Calvin," she says before we leave. "Don't fool around with tonight's homework."

The first thing Calvin

says to me when we leave the building is, "I hate that woman."

I tell him, "I think she hates you too."

Oops! I think. *I wonder if she heard me. I know she's inside the building and we're outside, but that woman hears everything. She has her ways.*

Chapter 9

ARF! ARF!

"Do you know what today is?" Calvin asks me the next morning.

"Of course I do. It's Thursday."

"Today is the first day for Calvin and Danny's Rent-A-Pet. After school, we'll go to Aunt Ruth's and pick up Mitchell. Then we'll deliver him to Mildred Foster."

This is too easy, I think. *I'll get two dollars a day just for taking a dog from one house to the next. I don't want to think about it.*

I tell Calvin, "I practiced riding my unicycle after supper. I don't fall off right away."

"Did you practice juggling?"

"I can do it with two balls but not with three."

"You have to keep practicing."

We stop at the corner. We wait for a break in the traffic.

"Oh," Calvin says, "Mom said she'll help you with your clown makeup and costume."

"Makeup? Costume? Do I have to dress up to be in the talent show?"

"Mom said getting you ready will be like decorating a cake. I'll also dress up as a clown. I'll juggle without a unicycle."

Being decorated like a cake doesn't sound good. And sometimes Mrs. Waffle wears strange clothes with different-colored stripes and polka dots and stars. I wonder what a Waffle clown costume will look like.

We cross the street and get to school on

time. We meet Annie and Douglas in the playground.

Annie tells me, "I'm going to the talent show on Sunday. Mom said she'll take me to see you and Calvin juggle."

"I'm going too," Douglas says. "I'm going with Annie."

This is not good news. Whenever I got nervous about the show, I told myself I won't know anyone there. Now my best friends will be watching.

Mrs. Cakel is standing by the door to our classroom. I bet she's surprised to see me and Calvin. It's the third day this week that we've been on time and it's only Thursday. If we're on time tomorrow, that will be four days. That might be the most days in one week since Calvin moved in.

All through the morning, I think about Aunt Ruth's dog and the Sunday talent show. That's a lot to think about. I keep

Danny, pay attention!

thinking this pet-renting business will not end well, and I still don't really know how to ride a unicycle and juggle.

I look around. The kids in class are putting their books away. It must be time for lunch.

"Danny."

It's Mrs. Cakel. She wants to talk to me. I go to her desk.

"You seem distracted. Is something bothering you?"

I tell her about Calvin and Danny's Rent-A-Pet and about Mitchell.

"Caring for a pet is a big responsibility.

You can't just take Aunt Ruth's dog to a stranger and trust that she'll take care of him. You'll have to go there often to see how the dog is doing."

I hadn't thought about that.

She asks about Evan, and I tell her how he's doing and about Sunday's talent show.

"That sounds like fun," Mrs. Cakel says.

"Maybe," I tell her, "if I learn how to ride my unicycle and juggle."

"Try to pay better attention this afternoon," she tells me. "Now go to lunch."

"What did she want?" Calvin asks when I get into the cafeteria.

I tell him.

Douglas asks, "How did she know you weren't paying attention?"

"She knows everything," Annie says. "I think she knows what we're thinking. That's why I'm careful in class not to think anything bad about her."

"She can't read minds," Douglas says. "No one can."

Calvin says, "My dad reads minds."

Here we go again.

"All spies can read minds."

Calvin says his father is a spy. That's why he's never around. He's spying in some far-off place. His mother says he's a truck driver, and one day he drove off to deliver some furniture and never came back.

Calvin tells us, "One day at breakfast, my dad said, 'No, you can't have a chocolate bar.' I didn't ask if I could, but Dad knew I was thinking it. He read my mind."

We finish eating, and Calvin begins juggling. Lots of kids and Mr. Baker crowd around our table. They cheer as he catches one beanbag after another.

"Get me an apple," he calls.

A third grader tosses him an apple. He catches it. Now he's juggling three beanbags and the apple, and as he juggles, he takes bites of the apple.

He's amazing.

"Go! Go! Go!" kids cheer.

"Clean your tables," Mr. Baker announces into the microphone. "Lunch period will be over in two minutes."

"Wait till tomorrow. You'll see my best tricks," Calvin tells everyone as he puts the beanbags in his pockets and finishes eating the apple.

"What will you do tomorrow?" I ask Calvin as we walk to class.

"I don't know. I'll think of something."

All during afternoon class, I try to pay attention. But it's difficult. I have a lot on my mind.

The school day is finally over.

Mrs. Cakel gives me another large envelope for Evan.

"Let's just give him his homework and leave," Calvin says as we walk. "We have a lot to do this afternoon."

We walk up the front steps of Evan's house, and before we can knock on the door, it opens.

"Maybe you can do your homework here," Evan's mother says as we walk in. "I even prepared a snack for you. That way you can stay longer. Evan really likes your visits."

Calvin looks at me. He's in a hurry to go to his Aunt Ruth's and pick up Mitchell. But I'm not.

Chapter 10

A REAL CUTE DOG

"Hey," Evan says as we walk into his room.

There are cookies and milk on his desk.

Evan says, "I can't wait until Monday, when I go back to school."

Calvin shakes his head. He can't understand why anyone would want to spend a day in Mrs. Cakel's class, but I can. It must be really boring and lonely sitting at home day after day and just reading and watching television.

"We can't stay long," Calvin says. "We have to pick up my aunt's dog and take him to someone named Mildred Foster. She's our first Rent-A-Pet customer."

"Will you come tomorrow?"

Tomorrow is Friday, and Mrs. Cakel doesn't usually give us homework over the weekend.

"Yes," I answer.

"You shouldn't have said that," Calvin tells me once we are outside. "We'll be real busy tomorrow. We have to put up more signs about our business, and you should practice for the talent show."

It's a long walk to Calvin's Aunt Ruth's. She lives in an apartment building a few blocks past the library. And Mildred Foster is a few blocks from there.

"This is it," Calvin says. "This is her building."

We walk into the lobby, and I realize I don't

know if his aunt is on his father's or mother's side of the family.

In the elevator, Calvin pushes **3**. We get out on the third floor and go to apartment 3D. The name on the door is Ruth Szenchecky. Don't ask me to pronounce her last name. I can't.

Calvin rings the bell.

Arf! Arf! Arf!

That must be Mitchell.

A woman opens the door. She's thin with long, curly hair, and she's wearing a very colorful dress. She looks like Calvin's mother.

"I'm glad you're here," she tells Calvin and me. "My friend Bertha is picking me up soon to take me on a mystery car trip. She won't tell me where we're going, but I think it's to visit her mother."

Arf! Arf! Arf!

"I like her mother and I like mysteries, but this car trip is no mystery. I once knew a mystery. She was in my class in school. Her real name was Terry, but we called her Miss Terry or Mystery. She didn't like that. I don't like spinach, but I know it's good for me."

Calvin's Aunt Ruth must be Mrs. Waffle's sister. They both talk like runaway trains.

"Going to sleep early is good for me too, but I can't always do that. Sometimes I'm too busy."

Calvin stops his Aunt Ruth.

"We're busy too. We have to get Mitchell, and we have a lot of homework to do."

Aunt Ruth introduces me to Mitchell.

"He's very sensitive," she tells me. "You have to hold him and pet him a lot, and you have to take him out to poop twice a day, in the morning and the afternoon."

Why is she telling me all this? She thinks Calvin will be watching her dog, so she should be telling him.

"Here's his food and water bowls," she says and gives us a shopping bag. "The biscuits are his treats, but only give him one if he's good. He can be naughty."

She picks him up and holds him with his nose almost touching her nose and — says, "Can't you be a naughty dog?"

Mitchell doesn't answer. I guess he knows that was another of those rhetorical questions.

Aunt Ruth attaches Mitchell's leash and says, "Good-bye."

I take hold of Mitchell's leash, and Calvin carries the bag of dog food.

Once we are outside her building, I say, "She thinks you're taking care of Mitchell."

"Not really. She thinks you're taking care of Mitchell, and you are, by giving him to someone who will hold him and feed and walk him."

"*What*?! Why does she think I'm taking care of Mitchell?"

"She knows Mom is allergic, and she knows you're my best friend, and since you'll be taking care of her dog, I can visit and play with him at your house."

"But I'm not watching her dog. Mildred Foster is."

"She doesn't know that."

I stop walking.

"This whole thing is wrong," I tell Calvin. "We have to take Mitchell right back to your aunt."

Mitchell looks up to me as I'm talking. He's a real cute dog.

"It's too late to take him back. We said we would take care of her dog and we will. We're just doing it by having someone else watch him. Now let's deliver Mitchell to Mildred Foster and get our twenty-eight dollars."

I have the note Karen wrote for me with Mildred Foster's and Jared Derby's telephone numbers. I wrote Mildred Foster's address on the note. Calvin is new here. He doesn't know all the streets, so he follows me. Her house is about six blocks away. We get there, and Calvin tells me to knock on her door.

"You're better at talking to adults," he says.

I knock on the door and wait.

No one answers.

I knock again, louder this time.

"I'm coming. I'm coming," someone calls from inside the house.

The door opens. A woman with short white hair and wearing a large apron is standing there.

"Yes?"

"We're Calvin and Danny. We're from Calvin and Danny's Rent-A-Pet."

The woman bends down and looks at Mitchell.

"Oh my, that's a cute dog."

"You'll have him for a week."

"Oh no," Mildred Foster says. "I called and left a message. My nephew isn't coming to visit, so I don't need a dog for him to play with. But I saved your telephone number. I'll call you the next time he comes, and you can rent me this dog."

Mildred Foster goes into her house and closes the door.

I look at the door, and I look at Calvin and ask, "What do we do now?"

"That's easy," Calvin says. "We call that Jared person. We tell him we have a dog to rent."

We stop at the corner. I give Karen's note to Calvin, and he calls Jared Derby on his cell phone.

"Here, you talk," Calvin says and gives me the phone.

"Hello?"

"Hi. I'm Danny of Calvin and Danny's Rent-A-Pet, and we have a dog for you."

"No. The dog was for

my son's birthday, and he changed his mind. He wants a video game."

Now what?

I give Calvin his phone.

I look at Mitchell and ask him, "What are we going to do with you?"

Chapter 11

~~~~~~~~~~~~~~~~~~~

A DOG BISCUIT
BREAKFAST

"We'll take him to my house," Calvin says. "Maybe Mom will let me keep him on our back porch or in the garage."

It's a long, quiet walk. Calvin must know our business hasn't worked out the way we planned, and he doesn't know what to say.

Wait a minute!

It wasn't *our* plan. It was Calvin's plan. Our business hasn't worked out the way *Calvin* planned. This was all his idea, and I got dragged into it.

At last, we get to Calvin's house. We stop

outside, and he takes out his cell phone. He calls his mother and tells her what happened. Calvin listens for a while. Then he tells me, "Hairy dogs make Mom drip and sneeze, and she can't drip her germs at the bakery in with the bread and cookies."

I look at Mitchell. He *is* hairy.

Calvin says, "We can't keep the dog at my house."

"What do we do?" I ask.

"We can't bring Mitchell back to Aunt Ruth. By now she's already in Bertha's car, on their mystery road trip."

I'm beginning to understand where Calvin thinks Aunt Ruth's dog should spend the next week.

In a way, this is my fault.

When Calvin said he had a great idea, I should have wished him good luck and said I was too busy to get involved. But I didn't, and now I'm in trouble.

We call my house, and I speak to my mother. She tells me a woman named Mildred Foster called and said her nephew won't be visiting. Mom said, "I told her she must have the wrong number, but then she told me about something called Calvin and Danny's Rent-A-Pet. What's that all about?"

I tell Mom everything.

She doesn't sound happy, but she says, "You can keep the dog in the garage. You'll have to take care of it. Don't expect me or your father to walk it and clean up after it."

She doesn't say anything about Karen, but I know I can't expect her to help.

"And it's only for one week," Mom says.

Calvin takes his books inside. He comes out with a big, white bag.

"Guess what," Calvin says.

I'm afraid to guess.

"Mom knew we were picking up Mitchell, and she baked dog biscuits. She used her favorite cookie recipe, mixed in some vitamins, shaped them like biscuits, and left them in the oven long enough to get hard."

He opens the bag, and I look in.

They look like dog biscuits, but they smell like cookies.

"Let's go," I say. "Let's get Mitchell to my house and feed him."

On our way, Calvin says, "You're really the lucky one. We were charging four dollars a day to rent Mitchell, and you're getting him for free."

"No," I tell him. "You're the lucky one. You were stuck with your aunt's dog, and I'm helping you."

Our garage door is open, and the garage is mostly empty. Mom has taken out her car. We lead Mitchell right past my unicycle, and I remember the talent show. This weekend, I have to walk, feed, and pet someone else's dog and practice juggling while riding my unicycle. I'll be busy.

I push the button to close the garage door.

Calvin takes the food and water bowls out of the bag.

Our garage is attached to the house. I take the water bowl into our kitchen.

Mom is by the sink, peeling the skin off carrots. They're for dinner. We always have vegetables at dinner. Mom sees me standing behind her with the bowl and asks, "Is that for the dog?"

"Yes."

Mom takes the bowl from me, fills it about halfway with water, and gives it back.

"Be careful when you walk with it," she says. "Don't spill any."

I hold the bowl with both hands and walk slowly to the garage. Mom is right behind me.

Mitchell is eating from the food bowl. I put the water right next to it.

"He's so cute," my mother says.

We all stand there and watch Mitchell eat. When he's done, Mom holds out her arms and says, "Come here, baby. Come to Mama."

Come to Mama!!!!

I bet that's what she said to me when I was a baby and just learning to walk. I don't know how I feel about that. Either she's treating Mitchell like a person and member of the family or she treated me like a miniature collie.

Mitchell runs into my mother's arms.

"You're a good dog, aren't you?" Mom says and pets him.

Mitchell wags his tail. That means he's happy.

Mom pets him awhile. Then she goes back to the kitchen and peels some more carrots.

"Here, doggy," Calvin says and holds out one of his mother's dog biscuits. "Here, doggy."

Mitchell runs to Calvin and eats the biscuit.

We play for a while with Mitchell. Even Karen comes in the garage and plays with him.

Calvin says, "I'll be back tomorrow morning to help."

Calvin leaves through the kitchen.

I look around. There are a lawn mower and other gardening tools in the garage, my unicycle, and a ladder. What will Mitchell do here all afternoon and night? What does any dog do all day?

Well, Mitchell doesn't have homework, but I do. I also have to practice juggling and riding my unicycle.

"Good-bye, Mitchell," I say and walk toward the door to the kitchen.

Mitchell looks up at me, tilts his head to the side, and wags his tail.

I hold out my hands, and he runs to me. I pet him and say, "I'm sorry. I have to go inside and do my homework."

Mitchell looks up at me and wags his tail. I think he understands.

I sit at the desk in my room. It's sad for me to say this, but I have so much to do today that I sort of "Calvin" my homework. I do it all, but I'm not careful to be sure every answer is right.

I still have some time before dinner, so I practice juggling with rolled-up socks. I'm getting better. I can easily keep two sock balls in the air but not three.

After dinner, I go to the garage to take out the unicycle. I need to practice.

Mitchell runs into my arms.

Arf! Arf!

His tail is really wagging. He's so glad to see me.

I attach Mitchell's leash and take him for a walk. I can practice riding my unicycle later.

* * *

I get up early Friday morning. Once I'm dressed, I go downstairs. I don't stop for breakfast. I go to the garage and take Mitchell out. Calvin meets me at his house, and we walk together. Calvin brought a plastic bag to clean up.

Mitchell stops by a fire hydrant and lifts his leg. I turn. It doesn't seem polite to watch. He should be done, so I turn. I wish I hadn't. Now he's squatting. Don't ask what he's doing!

Calvin cleans up. He drops the plastic bag in a large public garbage can, and we're done. We bring Mitchell back to my garage and fill his bowls with food and water.

Calvin already has his schoolbooks. I get mine and tell Calvin it's too late for breakfast. He looks at Mitchell eating *his* breakfast. Calvin turns and looks at his mother's white bag.

"It's not too late for anything," he says.

Calvin takes four of his mom's dog biscuits and says, "Let's go."

As we walk, I bite into one of the biscuits. It's good. I don't even taste the vitamins.

I sit in class and think about Mitchell spending all day alone in our garage. Maybe he'll try riding my unicycle. Maybe by the time I get home, he'll be real good at it. Then he could be in the talent show instead of me.

"Danny! Pay attention."

I try to, but I keep thinking about what's happened to me in the last few days.

I no longer listen in class. I have a unicycle and a pet dog, and I'm learning to juggle. I hardly do my homework, and I eat dog biscuits for breakfast.

I'm getting odd.

I'm turning into Calvin.

It's a scary thought.

I get home, and Dad is in the kitchen by the sink. He's making soup. We always have chicken soup for dinner on Friday night.

"I already walked the dog," Dad says. "I fed him too."

He turns from the sink and faces me.

"That dog is fun," Dad says.

Everyone likes him. Maybe Calvin is right. Maybe I am lucky to have Mitchell at my house for a whole week.

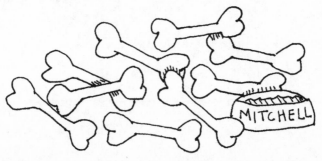

Chapter 12

~~~~~~~~

THE BIRTHDAY CAKE CLOWN

It's Sunday morning. I'm on my way to Calvin's house with my unicycle. No, I'm not riding it. I'm rolling it. Mrs. Waffle is taking us to the hospital, but first she's going to dress me up as a clown.

Calvin is walking toward me. He looks strange. One half of his face from his forehead to his chin is painted blue, and the other half is yellow. His shirt is also strange. It's a really big T-shirt, and large blue and yellow letters on it spell out "The Juggling Green Clown."

"How do I look?" Calvin asks when he gets

up to me. "Mom dressed me as the Green Clown."

"But you're not green. You're blue and yellow."

"Aha!" Calvin says real loud. "And blue and yellow make green."

I guess if he spins around real fast, the two colors would blend together and look green,

but right now, they're blue and yellow.

What will his mother do to me?

I'm a bit scared as the Green Clown and I walk to Calvin's house.

Mrs. Waffle is waiting for us by her front door.

"Come in. Come in," she says. "I've got great plans for your costume."

This doesn't sound good.

"I thought all yesterday about what sort of clown you should be, and then I thought that decorating you will be like decorating a cake, and I love decorating cakes. I love everything I do at the bakery, especially shooting jelly into jelly donuts. When I do that, I feel like I'm a doctor. Of course, if I were a doctor, I wouldn't give good children lollipops. I would give them cookies."

"Mom," Calvin says. "The talent show begins soon."

"Yes. I should stop talking and start decorating."

I follow Mrs. Waffle into the kitchen. On the table is a large cardboard box covered with white icing and small pink icing flowers. There's a large hole in the middle of the box.

"You're going to be the Birthday Cake Clown. You're a three-layer cake with buttercream filling. That's the best filling. It's much better than a tooth filling. But it's not really the tooth filling I don't like. It's all the drilling the dentist does."

"Mom," Calvin says. "We have to hurry."

"Yes, of course. Hurry, hurry, hurry," Mrs. Waffle says as she opens a tube of lipstick. She draws a large red circle on each of my cheeks and smaller circles across my forehead and arms.

"Hurry, hurry, hurry," she says and puts a cap on my head with birthday candles stuck to the top.

"Hurry, hurry, hurry," she says. "Let's go. I'll put the cake on you when we get there."

She puts the cardboard cake in the front seat of her car and my unicycle in the trunk. Calvin and I get in the backseat.

"I love to juggle," Calvin says. "This is going to be fun."

I'm not so sure I'll have any fun. I can hardly ride my unicycle and juggle, and I wonder how

I'll do it while wearing a large box covered with icing.

Mrs. Waffle parks her car by the pediatric part of the hospital. That's the place for children who are sick. We walk in, and there is a large sign announcing the talent show. It says the show is in the playroom, so that's where we go.

It's a large room. There's nothing in the middle of the room—just floor. Along the back are a few rows of chairs. Along all the walls are low bookshelves filled with books, toys, and games. There are a few children sitting at round tables near some of the bookshelves. They're playing games and putting together puzzles.

Evan is there with his parents. He's sitting with his broken ankle leg sticking straight out. His crutches are leaning on one side of his chair. His parents are on the other side.

"Hey! Hey!" Evan calls to us.

"I'm so glad you came," Evan's mother tells

us. "Your visits have been really great for Evan. Now we can't wait to see what you'll do in the show."

I *can* wait.

I wish Mrs. Waffle and Evan and his parents weren't here. I wish no one I know would be watching.

The show does not begin for another half hour, so I practice riding my unicycle and Calvin practices juggling. He's juggling jelly donuts. He has a whole bag of them. I forgot to bring things to juggle, so Calvin gives me three donuts.

Children begin to come into the room. Most of them are in wheelchairs. Annie and Douglas come in with Annie's parents. They sit in the front row of chairs. My parents and Karen come in and sit in the second row.

Now I'm *really* nervous.

"Welcome, welcome to our Sunday talent show," a woman standing in the middle of the room says real loud. "I'm Sylvia, and I'm excited. This will be a great show. We have many of our regular performers and a few new ones."

People in the room had been talking. Now they're quiet.

"Maria Johnson will start us off by singing one of her favorite songs."

A girl with long, dark hair turns the wheels on her wheelchair until she's in the middle of the room. She sings an old song about wanting to hold someone's hand.

The good part is she remembers all the words.

The bad part is she has a squeaky voice.

A few other children sing. Two boys tell jokes and riddles, and the only one I really like

127

is, "How many teachers does it take to clean a classroom?" The answer is, "None. Teachers have kids clean their classrooms."

That's true.

Now it's our turn.

Mrs. Waffle puts the candle hat and cake on me. I try to sit on the unicycle, but I can't see the pedals. I look down, and all I see is cardboard and icing. Dad holds me and guides my other foot to the pedal. I keep one foot on the floor to keep my balance.

"And now," Excited Sylvia says, "two friends of the hospital, the riding, juggling clowns, Calvin Waffle and Danny Cohen."

Calvin goes first.

He juggles three donuts. He goes faster and faster. Now, as he juggles, he takes bites out of the donuts. With each bite, jelly spills onto his cheeks, shirt, and the floor. The donuts must be his mom's special ones, with extra squirts of jelly.

Children in wheelchairs and their nurses cheer and applaud. My friends, my parents, and Karen also applaud.

The donuts Calvin gave me must be special too.

This is not good.

When I juggle and catch the ball, I squeeze it. What will happen when I squeeze the donuts?

That's a rhetorical question. I know what will happen.

"And now," Excited Sylvia announces, "Danny, the Birthday Cake Clown, will juggle while riding a unicycle."

"Are you ready?" Dad whispers.

I'm not ready, but I say I am.

Dad lets go of me. I pedal. I toss up one donut and then another. The cardboard birthday cake box sways back and forth, and I can't keep my balance. I pedal forward and backward. That's what you do on a unicycle.

I fall.

I land on the box, and the hard icing breaks off. The jelly donuts land on me and pop open. I'm covered with icing, icing flowers, and raspberry jelly.

I just lie there. What else can I do?

And then I hear it. Children are laughing—really laughing. A small boy in a wheelchair is laughing so hard, he begins coughing. A nurse hurries to him with a cup of water. My friends and family are laughing too.

Dad hurries to help me up.

"Are you okay?" he whispers.

"Yes."

Dad takes the cardboard cake off me. He picks up my unicycle, and as we go to sit down, he says, "I didn't know you were so funny."

Funny? Was that what I was? I thought I was clumsy. I thought I was lousy.

Children are still laughing.

Dad puts the cardboard cake on a chair in the second row. I sit next to the cake, and Dad sits next to me. Calvin and his mom are in the second row too.

I was nervous. I was lousy. But it seems that's okay because I'm dressed as a clown and people thought I was just trying to be funny.

I pick some icing off the cake and eat it. It's good.

"Thank you all so much," Excited Sylvia says. "This was one of our best shows."

I sit there, pick off more icing, and watch as children in wheelchairs roll out of the playroom. Some wave to Calvin and me.

Mom tells me, "You were really good."

"Yeah," Annie says. "You were very funny."

"Good show," Douglas tells us.

Excited Sylvia comes over and thanks us.

"Mostly, it's the same children in the show every week. It was so nice of you to come. You were both so good. I hope you'll come again."

Calvin, Annie, Douglas, Evan, and I sit by one of the round tables. We eat Mrs. Waffle's special jelly donuts and talk.

I don't say much. Instead, I think about life and how it's not always fair. Calvin was really great. I wasn't. All I did was fall off my unicycle and get hit with jelly donuts. But most of the talk is about how funny I was.

I tell Douglas and Annie about how great it is to have Mitchell as a temporary pet.

Calvin and Danny's Rent-A-Pet wasn't a complete flop. Because of it, I'm proving to my parents and even to Karen how responsible I am. Maybe after we return Mitchell to Calvin's Aunt Ruth, I can get a dog of my own. Maybe I'll get a big collie. Maybe I'll get it for my birthday.

We talk a little about school, and Evan says he's looking forward to the week ahead. He's anxious to be back in school.

"You want to see the Cakel!" Calvin says as

if he's really surprised. "Why would anyone want to see that woman?"

"I told you that when you visited. I like being with my friends, and I like learning new things."

Douglas says, "All this stuff about George Washington and the Revolution is not new. The fraction and magnet stuff we're learning is also not new."

Evan says, "It's new to me."

We talk some more, and then Annie's and Evan's parents say they have to go. The Waffles leave too. Mrs. Waffle lets me keep the candle hat and cardboard cake. I'm glad. I like picking off the icing.

In the car on the way home with my parents and Karen, I realize I'm also looking forward to the week ahead. I'll have Mitchell until Thursday, and I'll have my friends all week. I'll have them all year—maybe forever.

ABOUT THE AUTHOR

David A. Adler is a former math teacher, editor, and the author of more than 250 books including the Cam Jansen and Young Cam Jansen series, the Jeffrey Bones mysteries, the Picture Book Biography series, numerous math and science books, and books on the Holocaust including *We Remember The Holocaust* and *The Number On My Grandfather's Arm*. Among his books of historical fiction are *Don't Talk To Me About The War* and *The Babe and I*. Visit David at www.DavidAAdler.com and www.CamJansen.com.

And don't miss the books
that started it all...

DANNY'S DOODLES

The Jelly Bean Experiment

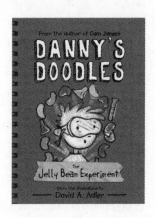

Here's a fact:
My new friend Calvin Waffle is 100% Weird

Danny Cohen and Calvin Waffle are two very different kids. Danny likes playing baseball; Calvin enjoys strange experiments. Danny follows the rules at school; Calvin tries to drive his teacher crazy.

Danny and Calvin decide to team up for the big jelly bean experiment. Will it lead to trouble? Maybe. Will they have fun trying? You can count on it.

DANNY'S DOODLES

The Squirting Donuts

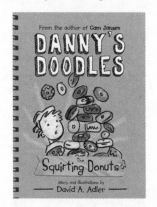

Here are two mean and nasty words:
Mrs. Cakel

Something has gone wrong in Danny and Calvin's fourth-grade classroom—out of the blue, Mrs. Cakel has transformed from a rampant rule-enforcer to a quiet excuse-accepter. Has she been replaced with an alien? Has she undergone a top-secret personality makeover?

Danny and Calvin decide there's only one way to find out what's really going on—**spy**. But spying soon leads to a greater mystery filled with dog chasing, jelly-injected donuts, prune butter-induced experiments, riddle mania, and more!